Hotwife Open Secret - A Wife Sharing Open Marriage Romance Novel

Hotwife Online In Your Local Area!, Volume 2

Karly Violet

Published by Karly Violet, 2020.

This is a work of fiction. Similarities to real people, places, or events are entirely coincidental.

HOTWIFE OPEN SECRET - A WIFE SHARING OPEN MARRIAGE ROMANCE NOVEL

First edition. September 14, 2020.

ISBN: 979-8201333232

Written by Karly Violet.

Hotwife Open Secret

A Wife Sharing Open Marriage Romance Novel

Hotwife Online In Your Local Area Book 2

Author's note: All character in this story are 18 years of age and older. This is a work of fiction, any resemblance to real live name or events are purely coincidental.

Be aware: This story is written for, and should only be enjoyed by, ADULTS. It includes explicit descriptions of intense sexual activity between consenting adults.

Note that this work of fiction resembles a fantasy world, all events taking place are a result of a role play amongst all parties and all parties are fully consenting adults.

Sign up to my Patreon account and receive exclusive Hotwife stories every month and sexy scenes every week!

https://www.patreon.com/karlyviolet

Chapter One: Coming to Terms

I pull into the driveway of our house and just sit inside my car for a few minutes. My mind is still swirling with what happened at Shane's house just an hour ago. Apparently Renee has come home as well instead of going on to Dallas. Is she waiting to have words with me? Maybe. Then again, what can she say that we did not already say in the way that we looked at each other when we each discovered the other's secret.

"Fuck," I moan to myself as I get out of my car and walk toward the front door of our house. Steeling myself for what might happen in the moments after I walk in, I reach for the doorknob and turn it to go inside.

The living room is silent as I close the door behind me. There is some music playing down the hallway in our bedroom, but I cannot be certain what song it is. Renee has been known to play music to soothe herself when she is angry, but then again she plays it when she is happy as well. What will she say to me when she finds that I am home?

"Hey, sweetheart," Renee says to me as she walks out of our bedroom and then comes straight to me. Kissing me on the lips first, my wife then pulls away and smiles. "So, how was the drive home?" I feel my heart flutter as I swallow hard. Her brown eyes look intently at me as she awaits my response.

"It was fine," I reply. "And yours?" My mouth suddenly seems to go dry as I watch the expression on my wife's face. She almost seems happy to see me and to talk to me right now. Where is the anger? Where is the fear? I saw and filmed what she had been doing behind my back. Surely that counts for something with her.

"I enjoyed the drive," she tells me as she has a seat on the sofa. Renee then pats the spot beside her and waits for me to sit down. "How long have you known?" she asks quietly.

"Known about what you have been doing?" I ask. She nods her head. "Well, I guess for about three weeks now. It hasn't been all that long."

My wife raises an eyebrow. "Then you don't know *everything,* do you?" She takes a slow, deep breath before telling me, "I've been seeing other men for about six months now, Brent. I'm sorry." Though she apologizes, I get the feeling that the apology is nothing more than lip service. After all, I filmed her with Shane and Adrian. Surely she has not forgotten that already.

"Six months," I reply with a grimace. "All this time you were lying about the work in Dallas?"

"Oh, no, I wasn't lying," Renee tells me. "Maybe stretching the truth a bit about when I had to be there and when I had to return, but I didn't lie about that." She puts a hand on my knee. "Brent, I have been needing something more for a long time. You do remember what happened seven years ago, right? You found me out and I begged your forgiveness, but I never stopped wanting to do that again. I wanted so badly to feel the touch of another man." My wife blushes a little as she looks away.

"Okay," I begin as I try to organize something coherent to say in my reply. "I found out three weeks ago but then I contacted Shane and he gave me a video with you in it. Honestly, it turned me on a little, but I was still angry, Renee. You should not have gone behind my back. We could have talked about this first."

"Talked?" She shakes her head. "You don't like to talk about that sort of thing, remember? I tried last year to bring up what happened all those years ago and you told me that it was all water under the bridge. You can't just shut down a conversation with someone and then expect them to talk to you later, Brent. That's not how good communication works." Renee seems slightly upset with me as she studies my face.

"I'm sorry," I say as I shake my head. "Maybe I should have been more open to listen. But, you still went behind my back. If I hadn't found you on that website, you would still be up to what you were doing and I would be none the wiser."

"A website?" Renee allows a wry smile. "Am I on that website?" I nod my head and pull out my cell phone. After navigating to the hotwife site where I have a membership, I pull up her videos and pictures on

Shane's page. She looks it over and even clicks on one of the videos with amazement.

"I know we shouldn't have been filming you, but he asked me to do it. So, I thought it would be a good way to get closer to you and see what you have been up to."

"All these men have seen the videos and the pictures?" Renee looks over at me, her face pink.

"They have seen them," I confirm. "Some of them have even left comments." I show her where the comments are on the page and she scrolls toward them. For several minutes, my wife looks at the comments pertaining to her sex videos and the nude images of practically every inch of her soft body. She seems a little taken aback at first as she reads the comments, but then Renee begins to smile.

"Some of these men really liked what they saw," she tells me. "I can't believe so many people have been watching the videos. Hundreds have seen me having sex with other men, Brent. Doesn't that bother you a little?" She turns her gaze back to me.

"Maybe a little at first," I reply. "But now, it makes me really horny to know so many men have watched the videos and probably even jerked off to them. They think you are the sexiest woman around, honey. It makes me hard to think about it."

"Yeah, I saw your friend standing at attention a while ago at Shane's house," Renee replies with a smirk on her face. "You should have just jumped into the bed and played with us, Brent."

I laugh nervously. "I thought about it, but I had to film it all. We will be posting the video on the website for others to see."

"Oh, the video." Renee looks hard at me. "Do you have it here with you?"

"I do," I answer. "But the camera is in the car right now. I sometimes upload at work since the internet there is faster. Would you prefer that I don't upload it to the site? I mean, it is a video of you with both of the guys, Renee. You can say no if you want."

"Put it up on the website," she replies with a smile. "I want to see how the men on the website feel about the new one. Maybe it will turn me on a little as well."

"Shit." Once again, I allow a bit of nervous laughter to escape my lips. "Are you sure you want that, honey?"

"Yeah, do it." Renee smiles at me as she gets closer. Her arm slowly moves around my neck and shoulder as she reaches into my shorts with her other hand. I am already hard as she pulls my cock out and squeezes it. "You have been a very bad boy, Brent. You liked watching and you liked filming me with those guys. The problem is, you didn't get to have any real fun while doing it." My wife bends down and takes my cock into her mouth, causing me to buck a little as I feel her tongue whip around my shaft.

"Honey," I say quietly as she pushes my manhood all the way to the back of her throat before slowly drawing her mouth up as she sucks lightly. "Dammit, Renee. Holy shit." I put a hand on the back of her head as she moves up and down along my hardness.

After a minute or two of this, Renee raises her head and asks me, "Did you like it when they fucked me, Brent? Did it turn you on while Shane and Adrian had their way with me?" She smiles for a moment before turning her attention back to my johnson.

"Oh, shit." I feel her hands gently massaging my balls as she gulps at my hard phallus. Renee is great at giving head. As a matter of fact, of all the women in college who blew me, none of them had the skills my wife has right now. She is great at sucking on a dick, and this greatness could be due to her other lovers in years past and more recently. I can even see where what I have done in filming her has helped to heighten my arousal for her and what she is doing to me right now.

Renee draws her lips up slowly and then looks up at me. "I want to do something else, Brent. I want you to be involved and have some fun too. It would only be fair for that to happen, right? Wouldn't you like to have a little fun with someone else?" She smiles widely before going down on me for a third time.

"Dammit, honey, I'm going to pop," I warn her as I feel my spunk moving from my balls to my shaft. I wriggle around on the sofa until I feel myself releasing into Renee's mouth. *"FUCK!!! Oh...FUCK!!!"* I spurt hard into the back of my wife's throat as she siphons my semen out of my cock. *"Uhhhh...uhhhh...uhhhh..."* Each volley of my manly gravy hits the back of her throat hard, causing Renee to gag a little, but she expertly swallows every drop of it. I close my eyes and grit my teeth as I finish coming and eventually she lifts her mouth from my spent dick.

"That was fun, huh?" Renee says to me with a laugh. "We need to do something to get you more involved, baby. Don't you agree?"

I look over at her. "Then, you aren't upset with me for filming you?"

She shakes her head. "You don't appear to be upset that I have been screwing other men, Brent. So, it seems that we are in the same boat. We need to do something about that if we are going to be happy in our sex life together, right?" Renee looks over at my phone. "Do you think we can spend some time tomorrow looking over the website and possibly figuring out what to do?"

I nod my head. "I have to work in the morning, but I can take off work early," I reply. "Maybe we can work on doing something a little different with the website. We could always set up our own account and show off or something like that."

"Maybe," Renee agrees. "We will talk about it tomorrow." She stands to her feet and offers me a hand. "Why don't you come with me and take a shower. We both need our sleep, Brent." I nod my head and get up to follow her. My mind, though still racing with all sorts of things involving the two of us, is now focusing not only on the past, but on the future of our sexual relationship together. I want to be able to enjoy sex along with Renee in some new way and I am happy to hear that she wants the same thing.

Chapter Two: Growing Interest

Work comes early for me this morning as I have a lot to do to catch up with what I missed yesterday when I left to go to Shane's house to film my wife having sex with the two men. As I sit at my computer and work on balancing the monthly finances for the automotive repair shop, I think about what Renee and I talked about late last night after we had both returned home.

"It just can't be that easy," I say to myself as I look at the computer screen. I have been having a difficult time keeping my mind on the matters at hand. "What is Renee really up to, Brent?" I ask myself. "Is she planning something devious behind your back? How could she be so calm about the whole thing? She was fucking dudes on the side and you were filming her doing it. That can't be all there is to this." I did not sleep all that well last night as I considered what we spoke about before going to bed. Renee seems sincere in wanting me to experience new sexual things with her, but it could be a trap. Maybe she is angry and simply not showing it. "Dammit." I shake my head as I try to get back to work.

My phone begins to ring and I pick it up from my desktop. Answering it, I say to my wife, "Hey, honey. What's up?" A chill runs down the back of my neck as I continue to think about what we have both been up to.

"Not much here," she replies with a short laugh. "The divorce case is over. They both agreed to the overall settlement and there will be no more reason for me to go to Dallas for the weekend. They are signing the documents today." Renee seems happy on the phone as she tells me about the ending of her case. I wonder what she would have done once the case had ended if we had not discovered each other as well as our secret hobbies on the side?

"Lots to catch up on here," I offer as I look at the computer screen in front of me. "I may be home late tonight."

"Not too late," my wife says to me. "I want to spend some time with you while we talk about what to do next. We agreed last night that we are going to continue on our little adventure together."

I smile to myself. "I'm not sure what that really means, honey. I know you said that you want me to have some fun with you, but doing what? Do we screw each other and film it, or do we bring in a guy or two? What you have done so far seems to resonate really well with the members of the hotwife website I showed you last night."

"It does, huh?" she replies in an almost-giddy voice. "I'll have to admit, Brent, I really like the attention I have gotten online. It's almost as if I am some sort of celebrity."

"Well, in a way, you are," I chuckle. "There are hundreds if not thousands of men and women who have watched your videos and looked at your pictures and enjoyed them. There are probably almost as many of them who have actually masturbated while watching your videos."

"That many?" Renee laughs. "Well, I hope so. I know it made me wet last night to see all the comments on the site. I even pulled it up this morning before work and looked at them again. They really seem to be authentic."

"They are," I assure her. "A lot of them also post their own videos and pictures on the website. Some even take part in threesomes and swing with other members of the site."

"Yeah, I noticed that," Renee replies. "There's a lot to see on the website and to do as well. We should talk it over tonight when you get home. Maybe we can watch some of the other videos and do a little mutual masturbation, sweetheart. You would like that, wouldn't you?"

My heart races inside my chest as I imagine watching the videos from the website alongside my own hot wife. It would be the sort of thing that would get me really hot if we do it.

"Sure, let's do that," I finally answer. "I would love to watch some of those with you. We can even cast a video on the television and enjoy it in high definition." We both laugh after I make the suggestion.

"Okay, then; it's a date." Renee speaks to someone in the distance before saying to me, "I have to go now. The millionaire who is divorcing his cheating wife is here to sign the papers. She should be here sometime early this afternoon to sign her part of the papers and then I will be free for the rest of the day. Get home as soon as you can, alright? I will be ready for you, sweetheart."

"I look forward to it," I promise as we end our conversation. "I love you."

"I love you too, baby." Renee hangs up and I put my phone down on the desk in front of me. Just two days ago she had no idea that I had been filming her with Shane and Adrian. It makes me hard to think of the secrecy of the act, yet at the same time I feel a bit dirty for doing it. Though I could justify to myself why I was doing it, the whole thing was a little wrong. I should have simply confronted my wife in the first place and seen where the cards fell afterward.

"Sorry to bother you," Kevin, one of my lead mechanics, says to me from just outside the door. "But corporate is on the phone. They want to talk to you about some new inventory that is on the way. Do you want me to tell them to call back?"

I look at the window where I would normally see the shop's receptionist and frown. She will be out of town for the next week or so because of a death in our family. It has left us all to answer the phone calls ourselves, which is not the best thing for a place where I need my mechanics working on cars instead of fielding calls from corporate.

"What line?" I ask.

"Line one," he replies before nodding his head and leaving the office. He closes the door and I pick up my desk phone to talk to whoever is on the line waiting for me.

"This is Brent," I say to the person on the phone.

"Hey, Brent, this is Lisa Malone," is the reply. "I'm with inventory procurement at Automotive Specialty Corporation. How are you today?" Her voice is smooth and practiced as the company representative introduces herself to me. I get a bit of a hardon as I smile to myself.

"I'm fine," I reply. "What can I do for you today, Lisa?"

"I'm calling about the new inventory shipment that will be coming your way soon, Brent. I just want to give you a heads-up so that you can make space for it."

I shake my head. "I haven't put in a large order recently. What shipment are you talking about?"

"It's this quarter's promotion. We are shipping you several crates of secondary items to push during the promotion period."

"Wait," I say with a strained chuckle. "What do you mean by *secondary* items? Are you talking about things like mugs, car fragrances, and such?"

"Exactly," Lisa replies. "We want each franchisee to sell at least a thousand units of each of the selected secondary items that are being sent to you."

"A *thousand?"* I push my chair back and stand to my feet as I try to comprehend what that means. "We have never sold that many air fresheners or mugs, Lisa. This can't be right."

"That's why I am calling each franchisee, Brent. We need to move these items to make room for next quarter's fresh stock. Demand has been much lower than expected, so you will be getting a handsome discount for the items we ship."

"But, no choice in which items I get and no choice to opt out of having to pay for them, right?"

"Brent, you know the deal here. We need these moved and it takes the franchisees on the ground to do that for us."

"Then don't charge me until after I have sold them. That would make better sense, right? Why should I store and pay for products that may not sell?"

There is a brief silence over the phone before the representative tells me, "You have a contract with us, Brent. You agreed to these promotional items before you opened your franchise. We are well within that agreement to send you items that you pay for and then sell. It is the way we do business."

I begin to seethe a little as I put my hand over my face. "How much is this going to cost me?"

"That's the beauty of this," she says with a chipper voice. "We are only charging you our cost. So, anything you make on the items is profit, minus the ten percent premium you will send us. That means that if you are shipped the air fresheners you will be charged one dollar for each one. They have a retail value of three dollars. It will be an easy sell."

"Shit smells better than those things," I argue. "I have more than a dozen out there on a hook that I can't get rid of already and you are going to send me a thousand more? That's ridiculous, Lisa."

"It's business," she replies. "Unfortunately, if the corporate office had to absorb every failed item, it would go out of business."

"So instead of corporate paying for their own shitty decisions, they push them off on franchise owners and let us eat the loss. How nice." I want to tell Lisa to go fuck herself, but I know that she is only doing what she has been told to do. There are bosses higher up than her who are pushing for franchise owners to swallow their terrible mistakes, and it makes me angry that I have to put up with it. There is really nothing that I can do about it, though. It is not as if I can divorce the company and move on with my own independent auto repair shop at this time.

"It is on the way," she says flatly. "Just make room and try to deal with it, Brent. I'm very sorry for any inconvenience this will cause, but feel free to take up your concerns with franchise relations." She finishes speaking and hangs up the phone. I put my own phone back into its cradle and shake my head as I consider the hit this will mean for my bottom line this quarter.

"Fucking stupid shit," I growl as I look out the window at the men who are hard at work. There will likely not be a performance bonus this quarter because of corporate's greed. I hate that for my employees, but there is nothing I can really do about it. My mind suddenly turns to what Renee said about getting home early this afternoon. I am not sure how early I can leave now that I have to figure out where to put the extra inventory they are shipping to us. Putting the inventory somewhere will be the most difficult thing to figure out. I will go home and have some fun with my wife after I have figured that part of the puzzle out.

Chapter Three: Mutual Agreement

Renee and I work to stream one of the hotwife website videos to the television in our bedroom. As the video begins, we sit back, naked and ready to mutually satisfy each other as we watch the images on the screen.

"She seems to really like what he's doing to her," my wife says as she plays with her pussy a little. I smile as my cock becomes hard. Watching Renee enjoy a video like this with me causes me to quickly become aroused. "I wonder if she liked it as much as I did?"

"Probably," I chuckle as I pull up on my cock. "She's wet, isn't she?" Reaching over, I put my hand on my wife's muff and finger her swelling clitoris. "You're wet too, my love."

"Yeah." Renee reaches toward my cock and grips it tightly before working her hand up and down its length. I love the feeling of her soft skin against my shaft as I move closer to her so that she can more easily reach it.

"Fuck, honey," I say with a smile as I look up at the television. The woman in the video turns and begins to suck the cock of one of the men with her. This is a threesome and both guys want some attention as she runs her hands along both men's cocks. "She's really into that, huh?"

Renee nods her head. "Brent, did it turn you on to see me having sex with Shane and Adrian?"

I laugh. "You know it did," I reply. "You were really on fire with them."

"They were good." My wife grinds her ass into the bed as I push a finger into her tight pussy. As I pull up, I can feel her bulging G-spot just inside. Renee pushes her twat hard into my hand as she grinds a little harder. "Keep doing that, Brent. It feels fucking good.

Smiling, I tell her, "I will do whatever you want me to do, baby." My thumb twirls along her lady bit as I massage her G-spot for her. My wife is turned on by what she is watching on the television screen as well as the way that I am playing with her pussy. Seeing the excitement on her face causes my cock to throb and ache for her. I would fuck Renee if she asked me to do so right now, but then it would become more about what we are doing than what we see on the screen. We both want to see what happens next for the woman there and her two lovers.

"Oh, wow. He's huge," my wife comments as she looks at one of the men's cocks. He is sliding it into the woman's ass as she braces for his girth and length. The other man is rubbing the tip of his own phallus in her face, covering her cheeks and lips with pre-come as he becomes hornier.

"Damn, I wish I was there," I laugh as I look over at Renee. "I could film that for them."

"They appear to have a cameraman already," she replies. "Someone is getting closeups of everything, Brent. They wouldn't need you."

"Then maybe just a third guy?" I joke as I smile. Renee laughs as she grinds harder into my hand.

"You're going to make me come soon," she tells me as she reaches up and begins to play with one of her nipples. "This video and your hand. Fuck, Brent."

"You are really wet, honey." I can smell her muff from where I am lying and I wish that I could go down and taste her. My wife has my cock tightly in her grasp as she moves up and down its length. I can feel myself getting much closer to an orgasm as well and I begin to thrust a little to oppose her motion. It feels good to have Renee play with my cock this way.

"She's sucking the other guy," my wife moans. "She's getting it from both ends." Renee begins to move her ass around on the bed even faster now as her body nears climax. "That has got to feel awesome, Brent. I want to be fucked in the ass like that while I suck on another guy. It's like she's on some sort of spit. Oh, baby." Her body tenses a little and I think for a moment that Renee is about to come. However, she calms herself and just enjoys the way I am fingering her as she closes her eyes.

"Oh, fuck...*AHHHH!!!*" The woman on the screen suddenly orgasms as the man behind her shoves his large meat deep into her ass.

"UHHHH!!!" Her other lover pulls her face back to his cock and shoves it into her mouth as she continues to come, her face becoming red.

"GAHH!!!" The man in her ass comes hard as he pulls on her hips to bury his manhood deeper into her anus. *Nahhh...uhhh...uhhh..."* His balls slap hard into her pussy as he releases his spunk into her. Some of the white gravy seeps out around his fleshy tool as he continues to thrust quickly in and out of the woman's asshole. *"Fuck...uhhh..."*

Renee and I then watch the other man come inside the woman's mouth and as he does my wife's body bucks a little. My wife comes hard, drowning out the sounds of the second man on the video. *"OHHHHH!!!"* Her toes point as she lifts her legs and spreads them a little as I massage her G-spot for her. *"BRENT!!! FUCK!!!"* Renee's small body quakes on top of the bed as she enjoys the burst of energy she is getting from her well-earned orgasm. Her hand stops moving along my shaft as she climaxes, but it does not bother me much. Seeing her have such a powerful orgasm is much better to me than a momentary satisfaction.

My wife finishes and then gets up. Her mouth immediately envelopes my hard cock and I lurch forward as I feel her suck hard. "Dammit, honey," I say almost breathlessly as I feel her tongue swirl at the tip of my dick. "Oh, fuck, this is so intense." I put my hand on the back of Renee's head as I look up at the television. The woman has turned to put the ass-fucker's penis into her mouth. She is not finished with him, as my beautiful wife is not finished with me. I feel my balls ache as I begin to shoot my hot sauce into Renee's mouth.

"SHIT!!!" The first spurt is powerful, causing my wife to gag a little as I coat the back of her throat with it. *"Oh, FUCK!!! RENEE!!!"* I pull down on her head and bury my cock as far into her throat as I can. *"Uhhhh...fuck...ohhhh..."* I come hard as I feel her continue to suction my manhood. For about a half-minute I enjoy the release of my man gravy into her mouth before I completely empty out into her. Renee swallows

everything before lifting her head and looking at me, her face red from holding her breath and satisfying her husband.

"You nearly made me vomit," she giggles as she wipes her face. "That was a lot of spunk, Brent. You must have been really horny."

"You made me horny," I say with a smile as my wife lays on top of me and kisses my chest. "You are so good at giving head, honey."

She smiles. "I hope so. I've had lots of practice." She rolls off me and then looks at the laptop on the table beside the bed. "Let's look at what we can do on the website," she suggests as she removes the link to the television from the laptop. I sit up as well and watch as Renee begins to click on links on the site.

"Do you want to join some other groups here?" I ask.

She nods her head. "Yeah, I was thinking about something just now, Brent. Something that I know we mentioned this morning when talking about what we could do here." Renee brings up a tab on the site that surprises me.

"Swinging?" I say as I raise an eyebrow. "You want to join a swinger's group here on the website?"

"Yeah, just to see what happens," she answers as she begins to put our information into an online form. "I want to see what sort of people are in this group and whether they would be a good fit for us."

"Wow," I say with a chuckle. "Swinging. That would be different. You do realize that I would be having sex with another man's wife, right?"

Renee turns and looks at me, her dark brown eyes focusing hard on mine. "Sure. And, I would get to fuck her husband too, right?" She smiles before turning back to what she is doing with the online membership form.

"This is definitely different from what we have done before," I tell her. "So, would it be something that you would want to film?"

"Sure." I am surprised that Renee does not need to take just a moment to consider the question before answering. "And we can post it on here, right?" She finds a video made by one of the swinging couples and begins to watch it. Both couples appear to be around our age and very attractive. The men are swapping their wives and enjoying them at the same time. I get hard again as I watch them together, and it seems as if my wife is a little horny again as well.

"We will have to link your videos to this membership portion of the site. Some of the other couples prefer experience of some sort." I point toward a statement on the members' page. "We can link the videos and still pictures of you. Of course, there is really nothing that I have to put on here more myself." I frown as I look over at Renee.

"You filmed them, so you were technically a part of what happened, Brent. I will put that into the application." She continues to type as she gets excited. My wife seems to be really into the idea of swapping partners with another couple. This in turn gets me really excited too, causing me to pre-come onto the covers of our bed.

"What will we do, then?" I ask her. "Will we advertise here that we are new and wanting to have an experience like this?"

Renee nods her head. "Something like that, baby. Let me worry about the exact wording and how I will put us out to the community here. Brent, I think this could be a nice new way to get what we each need and want. Something about the idea of swinging really appeals to me." My wife looks beautiful this evening as she spends time getting our profile ready for those who will decide whether we can be members of this section of the hotwife website.

"I will leave it to you," I laugh as I get off the bed. "I need a cold shower, though. Otherwise, I will end up all over you for the rest of the night and we both need our rest. I love you, honey."

She smiles at me as she watches me walk toward the bathroom. "I love you too, Brently. I'll see you when you get out." Renee turns her attention back to the laptop computer screen and continues to type out the application for membership to the swingers part of the website. As I walk into the bathroom, I think about what it would be like to enjoy another woman while in the same room with my wife.

"That would be very different, Brent," I say quietly to myself as I go to the shower and turn it on. "You would fuck someone else while your wife watches you." Recently I have gotten to see Renee having sex with other men. By swinging, we would both end up having sex with other spouses at the same time, which would be different, but exciting. I smile to myself as I get into the shower and turn down the temperature. I shiver a little as I look down at my full hardon. "Come on, give it a break," I laugh as I begin to just let the cool water do its job. Soon, I will be back in bed with my hot wife, so this may do little good. Ultimately, I will probably end up fucking Renee again later.

Chapter Four: A Serious Offer

Renee walks into the living room early Sunday morning and sits down beside me on the sofa. She is carrying her phone with her and she has the hotwife website's chat window pulled up. Looking at me, she smiles as she hands me the phone.

"What's this," I say as I look at the screen.

"A real couple," she replies. "Go ahead. Say hello." My wife elbows me gently as she curls up beside me.

"You've been talking to them?" I say as I look at the chat box. "Did they reach out to you?" I look over to see Renee nod her head. As I scroll through the few messages, I see one where they have given us their cell phone number. "Oh, wow. Are we going to call them?"

My wife nods her head. "I would like to. I wanted to make sure that you were onboard with this first."

"Sure. Call them." I smile as I hand back the phone to my wife. Renee dials in the phone number they have given us and then she turns on the speaker phone. There are only three rings before someone picks up and answers the call.

"Hello?" a woman's voice on the other end of the line says.

"Hello, Faith? This is Renee," my wife answers as she grips my arm tightly. "You asked us to call, so here we are."

"Oh, hello!" Faith seems so excited as she pulls away from the phone and calls her husband over to her.

"Hey, that was quick," a male voice says on the phone. "I'm Zack. Are you both there?"

"We are on speaker phone," I reply after clearing my throat. "My name is Brent."

"Hello, Brent!" The woman on the other end of the line seems particularly happy to hear my voice, which arouses me a little as I smile to myself. "We have been looking over your profile and we like what we see," Faith continues. "The two of you are new to this lifestyle, right?"

"Um, yeah," Renee answers. "We have been involved in some other things, but this is our first foray into anything between couples."

Goosebumps appear on my wife's arms as she pulls even closer to me. This phone call appears to be just as arousing for her as it is for me.

"So, the videos we have seen," Zack begins. "You are the woman in the video, Renee?"

"In the flesh," she giggles. "Brent did most of the filming."

"That's nice," he replies. "Then, you both have at least experienced a little fun with other people."

"Well, I haven't," I admit as I feel goosebumps of my own forming along the back of my neck. "I was just the cameraman for Renee and her adventures. We are looking for our first time to both enjoy our time with someone else."

"I see." There is almost an air of disappointment in the man's reply as he becomes silent.

"We really do like that you have been somewhat active," Faith tells us, "But we normally only do this with experienced couples. You see, we have been at this for about five years and we have found that the experienced ones are the best ones."

"Really?" Renee seems a little surprised. "I mean, sex is sex, right?"

"Well, sometimes," her husband answers. "We have met couples who were not yet experienced in this lifestyle only to have them stop what was happening and then walk out on us. It's really aggravating when that happens."

"Yeah, I can see where that can be a problem," I reply. "Still, we are a highly motivated couple."

"We can see that in your profile," Faith offers. "Maybe if you could tell us a little more about yourselves that would help us with any concerns that we might have."

"About us?" I look at Renee. We have already agreed to keep as much about our real lives as possible secret out of fear that someone might try to use it against us if things do not work out. Still, it would not hurt to tell them a little about us.

"I'm an attorney," she tells them. "My husband owns his own business. We are a very clean-cut, professional couple. Trust me, if we were to get together for something like swinging we are not going to run away from it."

"An attorney." That seems to pique the husband's interest. "What sort of law do you practice, if you don't mind me asking?"

Renee takes a quick breath. "Mostly divorce law. Sometimes a little civil injury law. It really depends on what the firm needs at the moment."

"So, you're not a criminal attorney?"

"Not enough money in that," my wife laughs. "Besides, most of the people you defend in criminal cases actually did the crime. I don't want that on my conscience."

"I understand," Zack replies. "And what sort of business do you work in, Brent?"

Not wanting to share so too much, I tell him, "It's a service industry type of business. I think that's all I can say for now if that's alright with you."

"I get it," he responds. "I work as an analyst at a large banking firm and my wife is a cosmetologist. We are also clean and very professional people, so it's nice to hear that you are both of the same cloth."

"Yes it is," Faith chimes in. "There are so many times we have come across people who are not what we expected. Their pictures show attractive figures, but then when we meet them in person they are not at all what they represented themselves to be. It's really frustrating at times."

"So, when you meet people," Renee begins, "Do you go have drinks and dinner with them?"

"Normally that's exactly what we do," the other wife replies. "We like to get to know someone in a casual, laid back atmosphere first. That allows us to really get a feel for them and whether they are the right fit for us. We also talk about what we expect in bed and how far we are willing to go. Sometimes that is a deal breaker for other couples."

I laugh. "Are the two of you pretty adventurous, then?"

"Very adventurous," Faith tells me. "I like a lot of things that most women do not like. When I am with a man, there are very few things I will stop him from doing to me. I'm pretty open for just about anything." My cock grows hard as I hear her say this. It is probably every guy's fantasy to have sex with someone completely uninhibited, and Faith seems to be that sort of person.

"We are pretty adventurous too," my wife tells her. "You have seen my videos, right? Well, there is very little that I won't do and Brent is the same way. We are very easy going too."

"That's good," Zack replies. "Still, I think we need to get together to talk about things before we decide to go to bed together. Faith and I don't like to just meet in a hotel room until after we have had some time to get to know the other couple. When would be a good time to get together for drinks and maybe something to eat?" he asks.

"Next weekend?" Renee offers. "Maybe on Saturday afternoon? We will both be free at that time if you can meet."

"We can do that," Faith replies. "Do you mind if we pick the restaurant? It will be our treat, of course."

"That's fine," Renee answers.

"Alright, then. Meet us at *Augustine's* at seven o'clock next Saturday evening. We will enjoy a nice meal and some wine, okay?"

"That sounds nice," I say with a smile. "We look forward to meeting both of you then."

"And maybe something more," Faith responds. "You sound like the sort of man I could have a lot of fun with, Brent. I hope that things click for all of us that evening."

"It will," Renee says with confidence. "We will see you on Saturday."

"Good enough." Zack is the last to speak before they hang up from the call. My wife and I sit quietly for a moment in our living room.

"They are definitely not convinced we are the ones," I say as I look over at Renee. "We are newbies and they are looking for people with experience in swinging."

"They sounded like they were pretty certain that they want us," she replies. "You have to have a little faith, baby."

"Trust me, I would like a little *Faith,"* I chuckle as I make a play on the other woman's name. "Unfortunately, I don't think Zack is very interested in us. His wife was probably the one who pushed to talk to us even though we have no experience in swinging."

"Sex is sex," Renee says while raising an eyebrow. "Whether we do this with them or with each other, sex involves the same thing. I think he is just a little threatened by you."

"Bullshit," I laugh. "That guy is sexually dominant, honey. I could hear it in his voice. He doesn't back away from something he wants unless he doesn't see an advantage to him. No, I think there is a certain sexual gratification for Zack in knowing they are with experienced couples over someone new like us. Faith is probably very excited for new blood, but he isn't. I'm not sure this is going to work out."

"It will, Brent. You need to have a more positive attitude."

"Yeah, okay." I laugh again as I sit back on the sofa with my beautiful wife.

"When we meet them, be nice and respectful, okay? That will win over the two of them, Brent. Just wait and see. They will want to be with us after they have dinner and drinks with us. Besides, they are paying, right? We have nothing to lose."

"I suppose that you're right. We can at least enjoy dinner and a little wine before they decide to drop us like a sweaty gym towel." We both laugh as Renee shakes her head at me. Even though she is a perpetual optimist, I often see things for how they truly are very quickly. Zack is not convinced that we are the couple for them and I cannot see how that will change during a meal. Though I want badly to have sex with Faith while Renee rides Zack's cock, I have my doubts about the chances of that happening. If it does, that would be great. However, we need to both be ready for the possibility that things could end without sex between us.

"Let's take a walk, Brent," Renee says to me. "It's a nice morning and we need a little fresh air." She stands up and takes my hand. I get up and we go to our bedroom to dress and put our shoes on. The morning air is a bit cool and we will need more than just shorts and tee shirts on for our Sunday morning walk. Hopefully this will help to clear our heads as we consider the other couple and what we will say to them next weekend when we have dinner with them. The air will help to clear my head and hopefully will give me a better attitude toward our meeting. Even so, I will probably continue to have little hope for getting to know the other couple as well as I would like to get to know them.

Chapter Five: Flirty but Not

The outdoor cafe that the other couple selected is very nice and accommodates the four of us easily as we are seated in the corner by the sidewalk. There are a few people walking by just outside the black wrought iron fence that separates the cafe's seating and the sidewalk, talking as they go by. I smile at Renee as she has a seat and I wait for Faith to also be seated before I sit down across from her.

"This is a really nice place," my wife says as she smiles at the couple across the table from us.

"We love it here," Faith replies. "Zack and I have been coming here for the last few years when we have decided to meet other people. There is a nice ambience here that is difficult to find elsewhere." She smiles at my wife and then turns her attention toward me. "You really are very handsome, Brent."

I feel my face turn red as I smile at her. "You are very beautiful as well, Faith." It seems a little weird to say such a thing to another woman, especially in the presence of her husband and my wife, but how else could I respond to her compliment?

"And you, Renee, are more beautiful in person." My wife simply smiles back at Zack, probably too nervous to repay the compliment at the moment.

"So, how long have you been doing this again?" I ask as I break the silence.

"Five years," Zack answers. "We have been with quite a few couples over the years."

"Around twenty couples," his wife admits. "We sometimes lose count, but if we could sit down and start naming them, we could account for every one. Some of them have been with us multiple times and they have become great friends."

"That sounds nice," Renee says as our server walks up to the table.

"Welcome to *Augustine's,*" he says to us as he pulls a notepad and pen from his pocket. "Can I get you anything to drink to start out?"

Zack looks at the young man and says, “We would like a bottle of California Chardonnay. Chilled with four glasses, please.”

The young man nods his head. “I will get that right out. Would you like any bread as well?”

“Sure, a basket of breadsticks, please.” The server smiles as he turns and leaves our table.

“Their breadsticks are beyond delicious,” Faith tells us with a smile. “I have never had anything quite as amazing when it comes to them.”

“I’ve heard good things about this place,” Renee tells her. “I’m not sure whey Brent and I have never been here, though. I guess there are just so many options in Austin that we haven’t made our way through them all yet.”

“This will be a real treat,” Faith promises. “The Chardonnay is wonderful as well.” She looks over at me, her blue eyes mesmerizing as she studies my face. There is a real connection between me and the other woman across the table. I can easily imagine being with her in bed and enjoying her thoroughly. However, I still cannot get past the way her husband is looking at us. Though he seems to be very accommodating, he is also not the warmest individual here.

The server is soon back with the wine and four glasses, setting the bottle on the table before putting the glasses in front of us. He opens the bottle and hands the cork to Zack. After inhaling the aroma, he nods his head toward the server and a small amount is poured into a glass. Zack takes it and inhales the aroma again before taking a sip. Again, he nods his head and the server turns to fill his glass as well as the others.

“The bread will be right out,” he promises as he takes the cork and replaces it in the bottle. “Enjoy.” The young man leaves and we each begin to sip our drinks.

“Very nice,” I say as I swallow my first taste. “Normally I’m not a huge fan of white wines, but this one is very nice.”

"It's a crisp wine for a cool evening," Zack replies. "Faith and I enjoy our wines when we go out with others." He takes another drink from his glass before the server returns with the bread.

"And would you like more time to consider your meal options?" the young man asks.

"A little more time, yes," Faith answers. Bowing slightly, the server turns and walks away as she reaches for a breadstick. Renee and I do the same, but Zack does not appear to want any as he continues to simply enjoy his wine.

"This really is good," Renee comments after taking a small bite of breadstick. "Wow. We will have to remember this place, Brent."

I nod my head. "I'll be sure to put it into my phone along with our other spots in town," I tell her as I pull out my cell phone and open an app. "Maybe we can come here for your birthday next month."

"Oh, you have a birthday coming up?" Faith says as she puts down her breadstick and takes a sip of wine.

"The end of next month," Renee replies.

"Well, happy birthday," Faith says as she looks over at her husband. He is still quiet as he studies the outdoor patio of the restaurant. "So, what do you both like in bed?" she asks after seeing her husband so reserved.

Renee looks at me as if I should be the one answering the question, but I wink at her to let her know I have no intention of saying anything yet. "We like just about anything," she tells the other woman. "Honestly, you have seen my videos. Practically anything goes with me."

"That's a good thing," Faith replies. "Zack likes just about anything as well." I turn to look at him and realize that he is staring at Renee.

"You are attractive," he says quietly. "But, can you really be a great partner while swinging?"

"I think so," my wife says to him. "Are you really worried that we are not up to the task?"

He sighs. "Faith loves meeting new people. Even the couples who didn't really work out were great for her. The problem for me has been that when I want to do something with the lady in the couple, the husband gets jealous or tries to control the situation." Zack turns his attention to me. "I know you watched her with other men, but you weren't exactly involved with another woman sexually at the time. A guy's mind can be changed quickly when his dick is in someone's mouth."

"Geez, Zack," Faith giggles. "Be a little more conscious of where we are." She looks around at the tables nearby. Though there aren't that many other diners nearby, there is the possibility that someone could hear our conversation.

"It's true," he says as he continues to look into my eyes. "Can you tell me for certain that you wouldn't stop me from having sex with Renee? I mean, if I decide that I want to tie her to the bed and really get freaky with her, will you get upset?"

"Tie her up?" I chuckle at first as I think he is kidding. However, I quickly see that Zack is being very serious.

"Tie her up," he says flatly. "How would you feel if I tie her up and just fuck her hard? Would that bother you?"

I shake my head. "As long as you don't hurt her I think I would be just fine with it," I tell him. "And would it be okay if I did the same with Faith?"

"No," the other woman replies. "I don't like being tied up. It's not my thing."

"Oh, I'm sorry," I say as I turn to look at her. "I would never do anything that you didn't want me to do."

Zack pours himself another glass of wine before sitting back in his seat. "I like things a little rougher than what my wife likes, Brent. Faith is the sort of woman who loves to be slowly made love to until both she and her lover explodes. Me, on the other hand, I get a little horny and just go for whatever I want to do at the time."

"And that's fine," Renee tells him. "Like Brent said, as long as no one is hurting another person we can do that."

"That's good." Zack takes another sip of wine before asking," Would you both be willing to go with us to a hotel after dinner tonight? We have a place reserved very near here."

"A hotel?" Renee looks at Faith.

"We have a room on standby whenever we meet another couple," she says to my wife. "You never know when things work out." Faith smiles and looks at me. "I think you would be a great lover, Brent. Do you want to have sex with me?"

I swallow a sip of wine and then put my glass down. My eyes turn toward Zack for a moment before turning back to the young woman. "I would love to have sex with you," I tell her. "I guess the question is whether the two of you feel that we are a great fit for you."

"A great fit." Zack takes another sip as he looks over at his wife. "I don't know, Faith. I'm worried about their inexperience and the fact that Brent hasn't been with another woman at all recently."

"I married Renee and I have been faithful," I tell him, "But we are both ready to take this next step. We aren't experienced swingers, but we are experienced in bed."

He smiles. "Look, I have nothing against you personally, Brent, but I don't feel like you really can let go and enjoy sex with another couple yet. We have been doing this for a while, and I have developed a sort of feeling for this lifestyle. Honestly, I didn't really want to contact you on the website anyway, but Faith insisted." This admission comes as a surprise to me as I am certain it does for my wife. I look over at Renee and can see that she is disappointed at his remark.

"It was my idea," Faith admits. "Zack sometimes doesn't act as quickly as I like, so I was the one to make first contact with you. He had already passed by your profile when I decided to message you."

"Oh." Renee puts down her glass of wine. "Then, we are a disappointment to you?"

"Not to me," Faith says quickly. "I think you would both be a lot of fun, but my husband is a little more difficult to convince." She turns her eyes toward Zack. "We were new to this at one time ourselves, baby. We could get to know them better in the hotel room."

Zack grimaces. "I don't think this is going to work." He raises a hand and the server sees him.

"Yes, sir?" the server says as he approaches.

"Anything they want, it's on me," he tells the man standing to his right. "Put it on our account."

"I will, sir." The server smiles and bows before walking away.

"I'm sorry," Zack says as she looks over at the two of us. "I really do like you both, but I can't shake the feeling that you are just not ready for someone like us. I think you need to look for a couple like you who is just starting out. There would be less of an expectation the first time around and I think you would enjoy it more."

Faith sighs. "I really am sorry. I thought it would work out." She drinks the last of her glass of wine and follows her husband as he gets up from the table.

"Have a nice dinner on us, alright? No hard feeling, though. You are both a wonderful couple and I hope you find what you are looking for." Zack reaches down and shakes my hand before doing the same with Renee. His wife then walks over to me, gives me a kiss on the cheek, and reaches over to take my wife's hand for a moment. Then, as Renee and I both watch with bewilderment, they leave the restaurant patio.

"What the hell was that?" I say as I turn to face my wife. "What did he not like about us?"

"I don't know," Renee replies. "Apparently he never really wanted to get to know us, Brent. He told us on the phone that he preferred experienced couples anyway. I think it was doomed from the beginning."

"It seems that way." Though the couple left us with the option of buying dinner on them, Renee and I decide the wine and breadsticks are enough. We soon leave the restaurant ourselves and make our way home.

Now that we have been turned down for swinging by Zack and Faith, we are confused as to what to do now. There are a lot of other swingers on the website, but we do not want to go through this rejection again. We will have to consider carefully what we will do next before reaching out to anyone else.

Chapter Six: Concerned

My phone buzzes in my pocket as I speak to Kevin at the shop about a car repair he is working on. I check the screen and see that it is a message from my wife but quickly swipe it away as I am too busy at this moment to answer whatever she has said. Though I hope she will wait for me, it soon becomes obvious that Renee wants to speak to me sooner rather than later.

"Are you going to answer her, boss?" Kevin laughs. "You know that she won't stop until you say something back to her, right?" He picks up a wrench as he moves around the car he is working on and I turn to walk back to my office. My lead mechanic is right, after all. Renee can be very persistent when she is trying to get my attention.

"Hey, honey," I say in a message back to her when I finally get into my office. "You know I'm trying to work."

"I know," she replies. "I don't know what to do." I scroll up through her previous messages and find what bothers her. Renee has been looking all morning at the website to find another couple that would be a better match for us. Unfortunately, she has had very little luck.

"You should be working, Renee. Don't obsess over all this."

"I'm not obsessing," she soon answers back. "We just need to get things settled so that we can find a couple to swing with, Brent. What are we really looking for?"

I sit down in my chair and think for a moment. Realizing that simply texting back and forth will take too long, I call my wife and wait for her to answer. "Okay, why can't this wait until after we get home from work?" I ask.

"You know this is bothering me, right? I don't like the way Zack just unilaterally decided that we were not good enough for him and his wife."

"That's his right," I reply. "Besides, I wasn't exactly getting great vibes from him either, Renee. We have already talked about this."

She sighs into the phone. "I think we would have had a great time if they had just gotten to know us better. We are a fun couple, Brent. Don't you agree?"

"Sure I do," I say as I sit back in my chair. "But you can't go off and continue to worry about what one guy thought of us, honey. It's counterproductive." Renee has voiced her displeasure with what happened last weekend when Zack decided he was not comfortable with us as a couple with whom to swing. I have largely let that go, but my wife is concerned that her previous videos might be turning swingers away. We have gotten some messages from other couples, but none that we feel are that encouraging.

"What are we going to do about it, Brent? Something has to happen or we are not going to be able to meet another couple.

"We are going to be fine," I tell her. "Honey, just relax and wait to get home after work. We can always go in and change up our profile a little if you prefer. I think we should probably add more information about what we want in a swinging session and how we could be the right couple for others."

"Our profile. I worked hard on that, Brent. It's not as if it was poorly written or too mean. It's a great profile."

"We need to soften it up a little, I think. Maybe we come across as a little too rough. We are new, after all, to this sort of thing."

"But I have had a threesome," Renee answers. "That's got to count for something."

"It does, but with the videos it might have been a little too much. There are lots of other couples on the website who are probably more reserved than what we have put ourselves out to be."

"So, we are overlooking a segment of swingers on the site?"

"I think we are," I answer truthfully. "We could be driving nice people away by the way we have put your videos right into our profile. Let's try to soften it up a bit and find out what happens. It can't hurt, right?"

"Right," my wife finally agrees. "It can't hurt. I'll start pulling the video links and then I'll write something nice about us. Brent, if this doesn't work..."

"It *will* work," I tell her. "Trust me, alright? We will make some changes to our profile and see what happens. Maybe that's all it will take."

"I hope so." I can hear voices on the other end of the line. "I have to go. The other attorneys just arrived in the conference room. We have a very important meeting about some things here. Hopefully I will soon be a partner here."

"You will be," I say with confidence. "I love you, honey. Have a good afternoon."

"I love you too." She hangs up and I slide my phone back into my shirt pocket. Getting up from my chair, I walk out to the shop and watch as Kevin works on a part of the engine deep inside the engine compartment.

"What do you think? Will we be able to get it back to Mrs. Taylor by tomorrow?"

Kevin stands up and looks over at me. "There's a lot of broken shit down there," he tells me. "What did she hit again?"

I sigh. "A large dog on her way to visit her sister. I think there is even some fur still in the front bumper."

"Yeah, there is," my lead mechanic confirms. "If you want me to get it running, I can do that. However, I'm not sure how long it will run with the damage she has underneath and just behind the engine. If I'm being completely honest, I need to have it here for at least three days to get things fixed on it properly. Otherwise, we are talking bubble gum and bailing wire to get everything together. I can't promise that she won't hit a bump and some part of the engine then fall out."

"Shit." I shake my head. "She can't be driving around in that thing, but at the same time she doesn't have enough money to pay for all of the repairs." I grimace while thinking about the elderly woman. She has been a customer of mine for the last few years and we have struck up a kind of friendship. I have always been completely honest with her about the problems she has with her old Buick sedan, but the old woman wants to keep it running as long as she can.

"Payment plan?" Kevin offers as he realizes my concern.

"I guess so," I answer while nodding my head. "She has never liked the idea of a payment plan, but I'm not sure what else to do for her. That damned dog has practically destroyed her engine."

"I'll tell her," Kevin says as he wipes his hands on a small rag. "Maybe she will take it better from me than from you. After all, you tend to be the biggest pushover I have ever met," my mechanic laughs.

"I'm not that bad, am I?"

"Your friend last month," he answers. "You gave him a free repair job worth two grand. If you keep doing that, you are going to bleed the place dry, Brent. Let me talk to Mrs. Taylor and I'll get her to agree to the payment arrangement. Then maybe she will see how important it is to get her car fixed." I nod my head and smile at him. Kevin will one day manage this shop and I will simply oversee it as the franchise owner. It is what I have wanted to do for some time now, but because of my refusal to let go of the day to day things, I have been very slow to move into that role.

"Take care of her and let me know how it goes. We have the Caravan outside so you can lend it to her if she needs it."

"Will do, boss." Kevin nods his head and smiles before he walks back toward the waiting room.

I begin to think to myself again about how concerned Renee is about finding another couple. Up until we met with Zack and Faith, we were both very hopeful to get into this lifestyle and enjoy sex with another couple. Unfortunately, things did not work out as we had planned. Just because we go to have dinner with someone does not mean that they will suddenly decide that we are for them. Zack did not like something about us, and maybe that was for the better. After all, we could have gone back to their hotel room only to find out that they are far too serious sexually compared to us. Renee and I are looking for something enjoyable, but Zack seemed fixated on something closer to BDSM.

"I don't want it," Mrs. Taylor says as she comes walking out into the shop.

"You can't be here," I tell the elderly woman as I go to meet her. "You should wait in there, Mrs. Taylor."

"This is garbage," she says as she pokes me in the chest. "Your hired hand says I have to pay it off over time and that it will take at least three days to fix the car. I need that car this afternoon, Brent."

"Yes, ma'am," I reply. "But we can give you our loaner vehicle for now, so you won't be without a way to get around."

"I don't give a shit," the older woman says as she begins to use saltier language. "Get it fixed today or I'll go somewhere else."

I shake my head. "Wherever you take it, they will tell you the same thing, Mrs. Taylor. I'm offering you a little discount as well since you are one of my best customers."

"If I am one of your best customers, you should get the work done sooner."

"The dog..." I stop as I look at the car. "How big was it?"

She looks confused as she looks back at me. "He was big, alright?"

"And you're sure it was a *dog?* I'm only asking because the damage that was done was by something pretty large. You have a huge amount of damage underneath and behind the engine, Mrs. Taylor. The car won't drive more than a few miles before you run out of motor oil and the engine seizes."

"It was big," she admits while looking from me to Kevin. Shaking her head, she finally says, "Okay. Three days, boys. Not one day more." She then holds out her hand. "Keys to that loaner, please." I nod my head and walk over to the desk.

After retrieving the keys, I say to her, "Take it easy with it, alright? No dogs or small cattle, alright?"

"Oh, shut up." I can tell that the older woman is about to laugh, but she holds it in. Whatever she hit was practically pulverized as Mrs. Taylor drove too fast down her street. I have noticed over the last few months that her car has needed more and more attention for damage due to impacts with other things. It might be time soon for her family to consider taking the keys away, though I would want no part of that shitstorm.

"Settled?" Kevin asks as he walks over to me.

"Three days," I tell him. "Don't push for any more." He nods his head before getting back to work on the car. I turn and walk back to my office to continue working on orders for repair parts. Hopefully the rest of the day will be less eventful than it has been this morning already.

Chapter Seven: A Perfect Fit

"Get in here," Renee says to me as I get out of my car. She is standing at the door of our home with her cell phone in her hand. "Hurry, Brent!"

"Okay, hang on." I close my car door and walk toward the house. My wife pulls at my arm and closes the door behind me before I hear a woman's voice on her phone.

"Is he there?"

"Yeah, he just got home." Renee points to the sofa and I go sit down. She sits beside me and holds the phone between us. "Madison, this is Brent. Brent, say hello to Madison."

"Um, hello." I am confused as I look at my wife. She appears excited as she winks at me.

"My husband isn't here right now, Brent, or I would introduce you to him. He is on a business trip and won't be back until tomorrow. His name is Kyler, by the way."

"Okay." I am still confused as I sit back on the sofa.

"Madison sent me a message on the website and asked if we could speak on the phone. We have been talking for more than a half-hour so far."

"The website?" I raise an eyebrow. "*That* website?"

"The one with swinging," Madison says over the phone. "I'm sorry that I am so forward. My husband and I are new to all this and we don't know what to say or do yet. He said to just go for it, so here I am." The woman on the other end of the line laughs nervously which causes me to feel strangely at ease with her. She has none of the experience or expectation of the previous couple.

"We are new too," I reply. "So, we don't know what we are doing either. How old are you and your husband?" I ask.

"Kyler is twenty-nine and I am twenty-six," she replies. "I know that puts us a little younger than you, and I hope it isn't a real problem."

"Oh, no problem at all," I say as my cock becomes slightly erect. "We just want to find a couple who wants to experience this along with us, whatever their age."

Renee can see that I am enjoying talking to the younger woman. She allows a wry grin to cross her face before she asks Madison, "What are you both looking for in swinging? I'm asking this because we spoke to another couple and then discovered we just didn't fit what they wanted."

"I don't know," she replies. "Kyler and I have been wanting to expand our horizons a little, so we thought it would be nice to do that together instead of just bringing a third person in who might spend more time with one or the other of us. We wanted things to feel more equal. Getting together with a couple seemed more natural."

"You don't mind having sex with someone else?"

There is a bit of silence on the phone before the young woman answers me. "I have never had sex with anyone else besides Kyler. I'm nervous about that, but also very excited."

"Never? Even before him?" My cock gets hard as I question the young woman on the phone.

"We met in high school and have been together this whole time. I've had sex with only him, so I don't know what it's like to have sex with another man."

"Shit," I say quietly to myself, causing Renee to elbow me sharply. She can see that my horniness is beginning to overtake me, so she decides to move the conversation along.

"What about Kyler? Has he been with other women?"

"One," she replies. "Just before he met me he lost his virginity to another girl. So, he's not all that experienced either. We married in college and have been together ever since. I hope that doesn't cause you to turn us down."

"Turn you down?" I laugh. "I think it might be a great matchup, to be honest."

"Ugh, my horny hubby," Renee remarks as she shakes her head. Both women laugh before my wife asks, so, what do you both like in bed?"

"I love oral, both giving and receiving," Madison replies. "Kyler is the same, but I know he likes doggystyle a lot. He can't seem to get enough of that."

"I like that too," my wife replies. "And do you think you could give my husband a blow job even though you have never given one to any other man besides your husband?" The question surprises me as Renee asks it of Madison.

The young woman clears her throat. "I want to do that," she tells us. "Brent, I will do my best to give you a fantastic blow job if we get together. Kyler says I am pretty good, so hopefully you will think so too."

"I'm sure I will," I reply with a chuckle. My face turns red as I think about what she must look like. I have not seen a picture of her or Kyler yet as Renee was the one to see the message on our profile.

"Could we get together?" Renee asks. "Would Kyler like that?"

"We would love it," Madison replies. "As a matter of fact, we could have you over to our house for dinner."

"Your house?" My heart races as I think about how easily the young woman has just invited complete strangers to her home. "You would want us to come there?"

"If that's alright. We have a nice home and I think it would be really comfortable for us. We can make a really great clam chowder soup that you would love."

"I do love clam chowder, but I haven't had it in a long time." I say with a smile.

Renee nods her head. "We can come to you, I don't see any problem there, but make sure that would be fine for Kyler as well. We don't want to show up unless you both want us there."

"He will be fine with it," Madison promises her. "He told me to set it up if I found someone. Oh, and we have a huge bed. It's a California king."

My cock gets completely hard as I think about having sex with Madison in her own bed. Most couples when they swing tend to go find somewhere neutral to have sex. They rarely go to each other's homes, as I have noticed on the website. As a matter of fact, it is generally discouraged in the forums. Since couples do not know each other, inviting someone into your home can be risky and dangerous.

"We can have dinner and talk about it," Renee tells her. "When is best for you?"

"This Friday? He will be home Thursday evening, so that will give him the chance to get some rest."

"And can we film us together?" I ask. Renee shoots a stare at me that causes me to shiver.

"Um, video us having sex?" Madison seems uncertain at first, but then she says, "I think that would be okay. We just wouldn't want it getting out so that our parents would see it. My father would freak out if he found out what I am up to."

"Understood." I smile widely at Renee and she turns back to the phone.

"What time on Friday?"

"Seven," Madison reponds. "Come hungry." She giggles a little on the other end of the conversation.

"Text me the address and we will be there," my wife tells her. "We look forward to meeting you both."

"Oh, me too!" Madison then addresses me directly. "It will be a great blow job, Brent, I promise. You will enjoy it."

"Great. We will see you then." We hang up and I reach toward my pants to move my hard shaft around to give it more room.

Renee looks at me for a moment before asking, "Just how horny are you for her, Brent?"

"I can't help it," I laugh. "You heard her, right? She really wants to give me head and I don't mind if she does."

"You are so terrible sometimes," my wife replies with a laugh. She gets up from the sofa and picks up her cell phone. "We have to get ready for

Friday, sweetheart. I think I want to bring something like wine to the dinner. It's the least we can do, after all."

"Maybe some of that same Chardonnay that we had when we were out with Zack and Faith?"

Renee scrunches her nose while shaking her head. "I never want to have that wine again. After they turned us down like that I don't want anything to remind me of that dinner."

I nod my head. "Well, okay. Then something else?"

"A red wine," she replies. "Something sweet and innocent."

"Like Madison," I say with a grin on my face. "I understand, my love. I'll see what I can get at the store tomorrow."

Renee sighs. "We have created a monster in you, haven't we?"

"A monster? I'm just a regular guy who is going to get his dick sucked by a woman who has only had one lover in her entire life, honey. That is huge for any man."

"Fresh meat, huh?" She stares at me before asking, "Are you tired of me, Brent? Be honest. I can take it."

I reach over and take Renee's hand and then kiss her on the cheek. "You know better than that, my love. I'm just excited about our new adventure here. I think we will have a great time with both of them."

"But, you will have a really nice time with Madison, right? She is younger and she has no experience with other men besides her husband. That makes you horny, doesn't it?"

Shrugging my shoulders, I reply, "And Kyler has limited experience beyond his wife. Honey, don't worry about whether I am getting tired of you. You saw how I was when filming you with Shane and Adrian. You're my hot wife and you always will be, Renee. There will never be another woman who will be as sexually stimulating to me as you are." I kiss my wife again before looking into her eyes. "You are everything to me, my beautiful and sexy mistress."

Renee giggles. "Alright, Brent. I believe you. Now all you have to do is make me some dinner and I will forgive you."

"Honestly? Dinner?" We both laugh as I get up from the sofa. It is actually Renee's turn to cook, but seeing that I am the loving and devoted husband, I feel obligated to take this task upon myself. On Friday we will enjoy a meal cooked by the young couple. Maybe Madison will offer me more than just clam chowder soup for my taste buds on Friday evening.

Chapter Eight: Dinner and a Drink

We walk into the young couple's home and are greeted by both of them just inside. Kyler is tall, ruggedly handsome, about six feet tall and sporting a nicely combed head of brown hair. Madison is much more petite, shorter by a little than my five-four wife, with blonde hair and brilliantly blue eyes. She smiles widely at me as she walks up and embraces me before stepping back.

"We are so glad to finally meet the two of you," Madison tells us as Kyler reaches over to shake my hand.

"We are glad to be here," Renee replies. "You have a nice home."

"Thank you. Kyler insisted that we get something bigger than we needed, so I'm not sure how I feel about it right now."

"We just moved in last month," her husband chimes in. "Maddie is still getting used to it." He smiles at her as he puts an arm around her shoulders. I watch as my wife looks over the handsome young man. There is a connection with Kyler that she did not have with Zack last week.

"It's very nice, though," I say as they turn to lead us into the living room. Renee and I take a seat on a large leather sofa while the other couple sits down in chairs nearby.

"We have a cook for tonight's dinner," Madison says after some silence. "I hope you don't mind that we are not cooking the meal ourselves. You see, Kyler and I are all thumbs when it comes to making a nice meal."

"I can make grilled cheese sandwiches," her husband jokes.

"I wish we could have a cook once in a while," Renee says while elbowing me playfully. "I would probably eat at home more often."

"We don't have a cook here all the time," Kyler tells us. "It's just that whenever we have guests over we want to be able to relax and talk to them." He looks over at a minibar nearby. "I'm sorry, I have been so rude. Would you like a drink?"

"The *drink,*" I say quickly. "I had a bottle of red wine sent over earlier today. Did you get it?" I did not receive a notification on my phone that the delivery had been made and I had forgotten to check before we left home.

"We got it," Kyler says with a large smile. "We can open that if you prefer."

"No, we can save it for the meal," Renee replies. "What do you have for a starter?"

He nods while walking over to the minibar. "I have a various assortment of whiskies. There is beer in the fridge as well."

"A beer," my wife says cheerfully.

Kyler nods his head. "What about you, Brent?"

"Yeah, a beer sounds great." He smiles and turns to go to a small refrigerator near the minibar. I am impressed by the setup he has at the side of the large living room. Maybe it is time for Renee and I to consider upgrading our home as well.

"Beer, my love?" he asks his wife. She nods and soon Kyler is walking back to us with four open bottles of cold lager.

"Can I be honest with you both?" Madison says after she takes a drink of her beer.

"Please be completely honest," Renee responds.

The young woman nods her head and takes a deep breath. "Kyler and I came very close to calling you and cancelling this evening." Her blue eyes fix upon mine for a moment before she looks away.

"Why?" Renee asks.

Madison sighs. "It wasn't so much Kyler, but I was getting cold feet about everything. I know I shouldn't be so worried about tonight and what might or might not happen, but meeting you was a huge step for me."

Her husband puts his arm around her and hugs her tightly against him. "Maddie gets a little worried about things sometimes. She doesn't mean to be that way, but she is naturally a very shy person. As a matter of fact, she is a bit of an introvert."

"Oh." I nod my understanding as I look over at the young wife. "You don't have to worry about me, Madison. I promise that I will be a gentleman. If you say no to it all, I'm fine with that. We should focus more on simply getting to know each other tonight anyway."

"Dinner first and then we'll see how we all feel," Renee adds to my comment. "Don't worry about us, Madison. We're nice people and we will understand if you get too uncomfortable and want us to go."

Madison smiles. "I really appreciate that. I think with some dinner and a little wine I will loosen up a little. Kyler and I don't want to be sticks in the mud." She reaches over to her husband and takes hold of his hand, squeezing it tightly.

"Then let's talk about something besides sex, alright?" Renee suggests. "What do you both like to do for fun?"

Kyler grins wickedly as he looks over at his wife. "Do you want to tell them what we do?"

Madison blushes. "You do it," she replies. The young man nods and gets up after leaving his bottle of beer with his wife. He leaves the room as Renee and I look at each other, our minds trying to sort out what he is doing. It does not take long before Kyler returns with a large black case. He sets it down on the floor before opening it and pulling out a large round object.

"What is that?" I ask as I study the object. It suddenly becomes apparent what they like to do for fun in their home as Kyler hangs a dartboard on the wall nearby.

"A dartboard?" Renee says with a bit of disbelief. "You play darts like people play in bars?"

"Yeah, but this is a professional set," Kyler tells us as he straightens the board on the wall. "Maddie and I play in here all the time."

"Darts." I smile widely. "How much is a professional set?"

Kyler looks over at me. "We have spent around five hundred dollars on this setup."

"What?" I chuckle. "You do realize that for thirty bucks or less you can get a set, right?"

"Not a professional set," he replies with some seriousness. "Maddie and I hope to compete next year in Ireland."

"Seriously?" Renee looks at the young woman and then at her husband. "That's pretty cool."

"I know!" Madison can no longer hold her excitement as she leaps from her seat and puts the two beer bottles she has been holding down on a small table nearby. She reaches into the large case and pulls out a sort of glove that covers only three fingers. Kyler does the same before they pull out a smaller case that contains the darts themselves.

"Tungsten tips for the best flight," Kyler tells us as he puts together his darts. "They are much less likely to bend when they strike the board and they deviate very little in flight." He smiles widely. "So, would the two of you like to join us?"

"Join you?" Renee shakes her head. "The last time I threw a dart I didn't hit the board at all."

"I might in a moment," I say after sipping from my bottle. "I want to see you both in action first."

Madison nods her head. "Let's show them what we can do, baby." She is the first to step up and carefully cradle a dart in her gloved hand. I begin to understand why only three fingers are covered by the glove. The other two fingers are used to hold the dart and throw it.

"Remember the basics," Kyler says softly to his wife. "Your stance and the grip is most important."

"Right," Madison replies. She takes a few seconds to measure up her target and then takes in a few slow, deep breaths. After a few more seconds she pulls back the dart and moves it forward smoothly, releasing it as her gloved hand comes forward.

"Nice!" Kyler exclaims after the dart strikes the board.

"It's too fucking out," she complains. Her face contorts a little as she looks at me and my wife. "I'm sorry. Sometimes I forget that we have company over."

"What's wrong? Oh, the *fucking* word?" Renee laughs. "We say that all the time. Trust me, you won't offend us, Madison." We all have a good laugh as her husband looks at the dart on the board.

"You are in a good position, honey. You can't always have a bullseye."

"I want a bullseye," she laughs. Madison backs away and allows her husband to take his shot. He does well, but not as well as his wife did. "You did that on purpose," she says with a chuckle. "Don't patronize me, Kyler. Do your best."

He smiles at her. "You know damn well that I don't play that way, Maddie. I'm cutthroat when it comes to this sort of thing."

"I'll bet Madison will do even better with the next toss," I tell them. "I can't wait to see where it lands."

The young woman looks over at me as she holds up the next dart. "Come throw this one for me, Brent. I want to see what you can do."

I shake my head. "I'll fuck it up," I tell her with a laugh. "I've played before, but it has been a long time. My throwing arm is a little rusty."

"Come on and help her out," Kyler tells me. "Maddie won't take no for an answer when it comes to darts."

Renee pats me on the back and I shake my head. "Alright. I warned you, though." As I get up from my spot on the sofa, the three other people in the room give me a quick clap. I can feel my cheeks turning bright red as I make my way to where the beautiful young wife is standing. She hands me the dart just as I get to her and I immediately sense the difference in the dart's construction compared to those I have used before. "Damn, that's nice," I say as I smile.

"Yeah, it's nice," Kyler agrees as he nods his head. "Let's see what you can do." I turn and take up a position that is nowhere near as professional as what our hosts used during their first tosses. I suddenly feel a small hand on my arms as Madison begins to coach me.

"Arm level here," she tells me as she runs her hand along my elbow to my shoulder. "You have to set up your stance too." Madison pats one knee and tells me, "Bring it forward just a little." I do as she says before she smiles and nods her head at me. "You have to feel like the dart is going to fly straight. Forget about all the shitty little darts you threw in bars or clubs over the years. They aren't worth the money they paid for them. Just take some time to move your arm at the elbow as you feel the way the dart will fly." Madison takes my wrist and moves my lower arm in a way that is a little foreign to me. "There you go. Just like that. This will be easy, right?"

"Yeah, right," I laugh nervously as I begin to try to aim at the board in front of me. I slowly move my hand back and forth, taking stock of the way the dart feels in my hand and where I want it to go. If I throw too lightly, the dart will fall and I might not even make the board. If I twist my hand one way or the other, the dart could end up too far left or right. There is a lot to consider as two semi-professional dart competitors watch me with serious intensity. I do not want to screw this up.

"Take your time," Kyler tells me. "Toss when you are ready." Everyone becomes quiet as I move my hand back and forth. After taking a deep breath and holding it, I toss the dart, my mind almost immediately convinced that I have screwed up and their nice wall is about to gain a new hole.

"There!" Madison squeals as she claps her hands. "I knew it! I knew you could do it!" She comes over to me and hops up, giving me a quick kiss on my cheek. As I turn to look at her, the young wife's face turns a little red.

"That was a great toss," Kyler says as he looks at the position of my dart on the board. "Closer than mine by a little."

"I had a great coach," I reply as I nod my head toward Madison.

"Dinner is served," a middle-aged gentleman dressed in a sharp chef's outfit suddenly announces nearby.

"Ah, thank you, George." Kyler looks at the rest of us and says, "Let's eat!" Renee stands to her feet and the young couple remove their dart gloves. They lead us toward the dining room where we will share a meal with them. We have begun to form a sort of bond already that Renee and I did not have with the last couple we met. This feels warmer and more inviting, so I hope it all works out. We will have to wait for dinner to end to find out.

Chapter Nine: A New Experience

"Wow, I have never had clam chowder this good," I say as I put down my spoon in the empty bowl.

"It really is very good," my wife adds as she finishes a bite. "We normally are not huge fans of food like this since we live in Austin."

"I grew up in Massachusetts," Kyler tells us as he pushes his own bowl away from him. "Maddie is from Ohio, so this was new to her as well when we started dating. I convinced her that it could be something that she would like, and here we are just a few years later." His wife's face turns a little pink as she picks up her glass of wine and has a drink. Though I am no aficionado when it comes to wines and their pairings with meals, I wonder if perhaps a white wine would have been better for the meal.

"Where is the chef? We should thank him for the meal," I say as I look around the dining room.

"He went home," Kyler replies. "We only hired him to cook and serve. It was expensive enough."

"Oh, you really shouldn't have done that, then," Renee says to the young couple. "We could have easily gone out or even just had finger foods."

"No, we would never treat guests that way," Madison replies. "Besides, we do very well for ourselves. It's not as if we are poor or anything like that. Kyler's work has brought in a lot of money this past year."

I look over at the young couple. "Would you like some more wine?" Reaching toward the bottle, I remove the top and hold it while waiting for an answer.

"No more for me," Kyler replies. His wife, however, pushes her glass toward me and I fill it again before giving Renee a little more. It is then my turn as I put the bottle to my own wine glass.

"You really do seem to be very nice people," Madison observes before taking a sip of her wine.

"Thank you," Renee says with a smile. "We like the two of you as well. The last couple we met were a little less relaxed."

"Oh?" Kyler raises an eyebrow. "You did this before?"

"No, it's just that we met another couple with the idea that we might have our first time with them. Unfortunately, they were not right for us. They got a sense of it and so did we. Drinks and appetizers were as far as we got." I look at Madison and ask, "Do you feel better about us now than you did earlier?"

The young wife puts her wine glass down and looks across the table at me with her blue eyes. "You have been very sweet, even letting me teach you how to throw a dart better. Sure, I like being around you both. The thought of what might happen next, though, still makes me nervous."

"I see." Though disappointed, I do not want the other couple to feel that I am an ungrateful guest. After all, we have had a great time so far, even if we do not have sex tonight.

"Let's do something, alright?" Kyler begins as he gets up from his chair. "Let's go into the bedroom and sit on the bed. We can just talk for a while and if things happen, they happen. If not, then it's no harm, no foul."

Renee stands up next. "Sure, that sounds like a good plan." She reaches her hand toward Madison. "Would you be willing to do that, Maddie?"

The young woman takes my wife's hand and stands up from her own chair. She quietly follows Renee as she pulls her toward Kyler and I get up as well. We walk toward the master bedroom and soon we are sitting down on a large king size bed. Madison is still holding her glass of wine and drinking it slowly as her husband begins to tell us about their sex life together.

"Madison can sometimes be a little shy in bed, so you'll have to go slow," he tells me.

"But, you seemed so eager on the phone," I say as I look at Madison. "Have I done something tonight that has frightened you?"

She smiles at me. "I told you that I could give you a great blow job. I can, but I will have to work myself up to it, Brent. I have never been with another man besides Kyler and I am worried that my inexperience will show a little."

"You are very experienced," her husband replies with a chuckle. "The thing is, your experience is only with me. That is what bothers you, isn't it?"

"A little," Madison admits. "I don't want to be judged too harshly if I do something wrong."

"No judgment here," I promise. "Renee and I are very easy going people. We understand. Really we do." Though I am sitting beside the young woman, I feel miles apart from her. She seems to cower in my presence and it worries me that I have somehow come on too strongly. If I have, I do not know in what way. I only want her to enjoy herself tonight along with the rest of us. That is why we are all here, after all.

"Let's start with what we are able to do more comfortably," Renee suggests as she stands up. My wife moves her fingers along the buttons of her blouse and soon has it open. Her small breasts, still covered in an off-white bra, are beautiful as she drops the blouse to a chair nearby.

"I can get into that," Kyler responds as he stands up as well. He unbuttons his shirt and then puts it onto the same chair as his muscular chest flexes. My wife is very drawn to his handsome form as she reaches toward the bra clasp behind her. Renee soon has this part of her clothing off as well and I feel my cock get hard as I watch the young man look my wife's naked breasts over.

"Take off your shirt, Brent," Renee says to me as she motions for me to stand up. I look briefly at Madison before I stand and wonder if this will be too much for her. After all, she has not begun to remove any of her clothing as of yet and the other two people could be moving a little too fast for her.

As I take off my shirt, I watch Kyler begin to unfasten his pants. His pecker is soon out and becoming hard as Renee looks at him. She too is working to remove her own pants and underwear. My cock becomes a little more solid as I watch the two of them enjoy the way they each look.

There is an obvious chemistry between the young man and my wife and it causes me to be very horny as I look down at my johnson.

"You are pretty big," Madison tells me as she puts her glass of wine down on a nightstand. "Come here, Brent." She smiles bashfully at me as she motions at me with her hands. I do as she says and when I am finally within reach she carefully takes hold of my shaft with one of her small, soft hands. "Are you turned on by this?"

"Yeah, a little," I say with a bit of laughter. "Are you turned on at all?"

"Maybe," she answers as she begins to run her hand along my cock. I feel my shaft inflate even more as I watch Madison's hand on it. Though she still seems a little apprehensive about doing much with me, the young wife truly appears happy to see that I am hard.

"Can you show him your breasts, baby?" Kyler asks his wife as he turns and smiles. This is the first time he has seen Madison's hand on another man's hard manhood.

"I'll try." She takes her hand away from me and begins to unbutton her own blouse. Madison pulls it away and then places it on the floor nearby. "I can't take off my bra yet," she tells me as I look down at the soft orbs hiding just within the light blue fabric.

"It's okay," I answer as she reaches her hand toward my cock once again. This time, she pumps my shaft a couple of times before leaning forward and kissing the tip of my dick. "Oh, wow." The young woman then slowly parts her lips and takes in about half of my cock as I feel her tongue lap at the underside of it. "That's nice."

"She takes a while to warm up, but she is really good at that," Kyler tells me as my wife reaches for his cock. Renee pulls on his manhood a little and he hardens while kissing her. I smile as I realize that we are at least soft-swinging at the moment. Even if I do not get to have full sex with Madison, the blow job she is giving me just now is amazing.

"Shit, Madison," I groan as she seats my cock far into the back of her throat. My ball sack lightly taps her chin as she swallows gently, causing a suction on my cock that is different than any other blow job I have experienced before. “Damn.” I run my fingers through her blonde hair and simply enjoy the service she is giving me at this moment. There is no reason to get into any hurry as Madison services me.

Renee lies back on the bed and Kyler pushes her legs back. He inhales her essence before lapping at her moist, sweet twat. Smiling, I think about how attractive Renee is and how badly she wants to fuck the young man who is eating her out. My wife loves having sex with other men and when she first saw Kyler’s picture in the message we received from then, she became excited. They look good together as the young man pushes her legs back, causing Renee’s lotus to bloom right in front of him.

“You are so sexy,” he tells my wife before nipping at her clitoris. His lips tightly hold her lady bit as he pulls on it gently. Renee’s clit stretches a little and then snaps back as it slips from Kyler’s lips. He grips it again and does the same several times as he plays with her.

“You are fucking teasing me,” Renee grunts as Madison’s husband reaches for her perky nipples. Flicking each one a few times, he causes my wife’s small body to move around on the bed. She loves the feeling of someone playing with her nipples and pussy at the same time.

“Are you okay?” I look down as Madison smiles shyly at me. “I mean, am I doing it alright for you?”

“You are great,” I answer as I run my hand along the side of her face. “I would love to see your breasts, though.” Madison’s face turns pink as she looks down at herself. It is my guess that she has not shown off her chest to any other man since marrying Kyler. Because of this, showing her breasts to me now must be a little difficult for her.

“I’ll do it,” she finally says to me as she releases my cock. Madison reaches behind her back and carefully unfastens her bra. Pulling it forward, she allows the bra straps to drop to her elbows. Even so, her hands remain over her breasts.

“You don’t have to show them to me if you don’t want to,” I say with as much understanding as I can muster. I want so badly to see them, but there is no reason to cause Madison so much concern.

"No, I want you to see them," she finally tells me. She slowly moves her hands and her bra drops to the floor. Madison's breasts are slightly larger than Renee's and her nipples are round and hard. I reach out and want to touch them, but I stop and look at her. The young wife nods her head and I go ahead and take them into my hand.

"You are so beautiful," I say as I bend toward her. Madison turns and kisses me on the lips as I play with her firm mammaries. I kiss her back and feel my cock pre-come as I realize that she is about ready for our time in bed together. Helping her to stand up, I pull at her pants and she helps me to get them down. Her panties soon follow and her bare muff is now within reach as I run my fingers along her delicate cleft.

"Fuck, you feel so good inside me, Kyler," Renee says to her lover on the other side of the bed. He is thrusting his manhood in and out of my wife's pussy as her feet are on his broad shoulders.

"Fuck me too," I hear Madison's soft voice say to me. She lies down beside my wife and opens up her legs to reveal her beautiful pussy. I bend down and kiss it for a moment as I enjoy the aroma of her beautiful pecan. "Brent," the young woman pleads as I begin to lick her valley. She tastes sweet as I eat her muff and I wonder if she might be fertile. I do not care, really, but it is something to consider after the many conversations I have had with Renee about fertility and cervical fluid. Apparently, a woman is often fertile when she has sweetly flavored pussy juices. It could be that I will plant my seed inside this young woman if I come inside her. The thought of this makes me harder as I push my tongue into her vagina to collect more of her nectar.

"Holy shit, Renee," Kyler says to my wife as he plows her field. My wife is a great fuck, and even a younger man like him can see how wonderful she is.

"Brent, you are so..." Madison stops as she enjoys the way I lick her clit. It is larger by a little than my wife's, so I use my tongue to investigate how large it can become. "Oh, my...*ohhhh!!!*" Her small body suddenly tenses as I take hold of her nipples with my fingers and play with them.

"Brent...Brent..." Though she is orgasming, Madison is very controlled in the way that she allows herself to climax with me. *"Fuck...ohhhh..."* Her labia turns almost purple as she points her toes and comes with my tongue on her clit. The fact that she is so reserved makes me even hornier as I pull my lips away from her wet snapper.

"Lie down," she says as she looks at me. "Here." Madison moves and has me lie down where she was laying just a moment earlier. After I do, she lowers her mouth to my johnson once again.

"Huhhhh!!!" Kyler's face turns red as he comes hard inside my wife's cunt. *"FUCK!!! OHHHHH!!!"* He slams his cock and balls hard into her as he empties his jism into Renee's tight, warm pussy. She smiles at him as she enjoys the feeling of his warm streams of semen inside her. *"Ohhh...uhhh...fuck...uhhhh..."*

Madison lifts her mouth from my cock and then moves to where her crotch is over mine. She reaches down and holds my hard member with her hand as she lowers her hole over it. The young woman's tight pussy soon swallows my cock and I reach up to play with her beautiful round breasts.

"You're deep," she tells me. "But I want you deeper." The young wife lies back a little and I can feel her cervix rub against my hard cock.

"Uhhh..." I grit my teeth as she grinds into me hard, her tongue licking her lips as if she has just had something delicious to eat.

"Kyler," I hear my wife say to him. She directs him to lie down beside me and in very much the same way as Madison, she goes down on him. Renee sucks on the young man to help him get his hardon back as she uses a hand to play with his balls. I watch my wife at work as Madison rides my cock for me.

Madison begins to move faster up and down my cock as she puts her hands on my knees. "You're only the second man I have ever fucked," the young woman tells me. "I'm so glad that you're fucking me, Brent," she says with a huff. "Kyler, thank you for talking me into this."

Her husband looks over at her. "We talked each other into this." My wife straddles his cock and soon she is sitting down on him as well. "This is so unreal," he tells her.

"I'm going to make you come a lot harder," Renee tells him as she bends down and kisses him, her ass moving up and down.

"You're sweet," I tell the young woman as I get closer to coming. "Are you fertile?"

My wife looks over at me. "She tasted sweet?" Renee then turns her attention to the young woman riding me. "Do you keep track of your ovulation?"

"No," Madison admits as she goes up and down. "I don't use birth control anymore either. Kyler and I are trying to get pregnant." Her body shudders as her vagina squeezes my cock hard. "Fuck it, I don't care. "Fuck...*ohhhh...*" The other man's wife is a little louder this time as she comes and I feel her cervix bouncing hard on the tip of my cock. *"Uhhhh...FUCK!!! OHHHH!!!"* Madison grinds around on top of me as she moves up and down hard. The constant motion as I ram into her cervix brings me to the brink as well as I grip her ass hard.

"Ohhhhh..." I spurt hard into Madison's tight hole as she continues to ride me hard. *"SHITTTT!!! FUCK!!!"* Suddenly, the thought of getting her pregnant overwhelms me a little and I wish we had done something to keep from taking such a risk. It is too late now as I deliver the contents of my balls deep inside her vagina. *"Uhhh...fuck...uhhhh...ohhhhh..."*

"FUCK!!!" Kyler comes for a second time and spurts hard inside my wife. *"Oh, SHIT! FUCK!"* He holds tightly to her small breasts as he empties into her and kisses Renee before she leans back a little.

"Kyler...OHHHH..." My wife's orgasm is powerful as she moves her ass and pussy against the young man's body. Squirting a little, she makes a mess on Kyler that he has probably not had before. I smile as I finish coming inside my own lover. That has to be a surprise to the other man as she showers him with her juices. *"UHHHH!!! UHHHH!!!"*

There is a thick smell of sex in the air as we all finish orgasming. To my delight, Madison simply lays down on me and allows me to keep my cock inside her pussy for a while as she kisses my chest. The once-bashful woman is no longer so keen on getting away from me. We all four lie on the bed for a while as silence fills the room. There is little to say to one another as we simply enjoy the moment. This is something that we have all wanted and now that it has happened we do not want it to end.

Chapter Ten: Breakfast Among Friends

"Good morning, sleepyhead," I say to Renee as I smile at her. She has slept in far later than the rest of us after our night of sex together. Kyler has offered to make us pancakes this morning and Madison is sitting close to me as her fingers move through my hair.

"I'm sorry that I didn't get up sooner," she replies. "I think I was just so worn out from last night."

"My fault," Kyler says with a wicked smile. Renee smiles as well as I enjoy the feeling of Madison's fingers moving through my hair.

"So, what's next?" I say with a smile at the others in the kitchen. We spent all night together, with Madison and I retreating to a spare bedroom next door to enjoy our time with each other. I came at least twice more with the young woman before three o'clock this morning when we finally fell asleep in each other's arms.

"That's a good question," Kyler responds. "I think Maddie and I have become very comfortable with you both. I would like to see us spend more time together, if that is something the two of you would be willing to do."

"I like that idea," Renee replies. "This was so much easier than what I thought it would be. Everything seemed so natural." My wife looks over at her most recent lover as she takes a sip of hot coffee from a cup he has just handed her.

"Then we should get together again." Madison's fingers run down my neck and then my back as I say this. "But we don't need to simply lock ourselves into being mutually exclusive."

"No, but I think I'm going to have a hard time doing this with anyone else," Madison replies. "I understand, though. Swinging is more than just trading a partner with one couple for the rest of your life. It's a lifestyle that needs to be explored further."

Kyler nods his head. "Still, if you want to get together again, I think Maddie and I would be happy with that."

Renee looks at me before she says, "Brent and I would love that. We just want to keep our options open as well." She takes another sip before asking, "What do we do for the rest of the day?"

"Hiking," Madison answers quickly. "And then, who knows what? The woods are a great place to get freaky."

I laugh while shaking my head. "A freaky hike in the woods, then. I like it." We all laugh as we continue to enjoy one another's company. This has worked out well for us so far and I want to develop a deep friendship with the other couple. That does not mean that Renee and I do not have sex with others. That will continue to be a part of our relationship. Now, though, it appears that our sexual desires could lead into any direction. We have to be ready to move in whatever way things open up for us.

TO BE CONTINUED

Sign up to my Patreon account and receive exclusive Hotwife stories every month and sexy scenes every week!

https://www.patreon.com/karlyviolet

Don't miss out!

Visit the website below and you can sign up to receive emails whenever Karly Violet publishes a new book. There's no charge and no obligation.

https://books2read.com/r/B-A-GIXE-VSFIB

BOOKS 2 READ

Connecting independent readers to independent writers.

Did you love *Hotwife Open Secret - A Wife Sharing Open Marriage Romance Novel*? Then you should read *Hotwife In The Strip Club - A Wife watching Hot Wife Turned Stripper Open Relationship Romance Novel*[1] by Karly Violet!

[2]

Wife Turns Stripper When The Financial Woes Stack Up!

Branden and Lindsey have hit the dreaded tough financial times.

The worried husband's day job hasn't rewarded him with the increase in pay and the beautiful wife's job in the day spa just doesn't pay enough.

And as with any debt dilemma, things start to go from bad to worse each month.

Lindsey's closest friend is all too familiar with making money at a gentlemen's club, exposing her body for the drooling men loaded with cash.

---

1. https://books2read.com/u/mKwE0P

2. https://books2read.com/u/mKwE0P

And so when the idea pops into the desperate wife's head.....

......husband and wife are prepared to try almost anything things as......

Lindsey strips down and gyrates on the pole to clear the mounting debts!!!

This scorching hot 20k word novel is features a beautiful hotwife stripping down in front of thirsty crowd at a gentleman's club to earn some much needed cash for her marriage.

Read more at https://www.patreon.com/karlyviolet.

About the Author

Sign up to my mailing list to receive the two free epilogues for 'A Hotwife Adventure' and 'Hotwife Training' and to stay up to date on all of my latest releases! http://eepurl.com/c3ICWf Sign up to my Patreon account and receive exclusive Hotwife stories every month and sexy scenes every week! https://www.patreon.com/karlyviolet

Read more at https://www.patreon.com/karlyviolet.

About the Publisher

www.ingramcontent.com/pod-product-compliance
Ingram Content Group UK Ltd.
Pitfield, Milton Keynes, MK11 3LW, UK
UKHW041822200726
13854UKWH00001BA/445